The homes we live in

Sally Hewitt and Jane Rowe

Evans

About this book

The LOOK AROUND YOU books have been put together in a way that makes them ideal for teachers and parents to share with young children. Take time over each question and project. Have fun learning about how all sorts of different homes, clothes, toys and everyday objects have been designed for a special purpose.

THE HOMES WE LIVE In deals with the kinds of ideas about design and technology that many children will be introduced to in their early years at school. The pictures and text will encourage children to explore design on the page, and all around them. This book will help them to understand why their homes, furniture and decoration are made from particular materials, have a certain shape, size, pattern and work well. It will also help them to develop their own design skills.

The 'eye opener' boxes reveal interesting and unusual facts, or lead children to examine one aspect of design. There are also activities that put theory into practice in an entertaining and informative way. Children learn most effectively by joining in, talking, asking questions and solving problems, so encourage them to talk about what they are doing and to find ways of solving the problems for themselves.

Try to make thinking about design and technology a part of everyday life. Just pick up any object around the house and talk about why it has been made that way, and how it could be improved. Design is not just a subject for adults. You can have a lot of fun with it at any age - and develop artistic flair and practical skills.

Contents

The homes we live in

What is a **home?** Your home is where you live with your **family**.

It shelters you and keeps you **safe**.

It is where you keep your things and **play** with your **friends**.

Every home is **different**.
You can choose furniture,
pictures and colours to make
a home into your
own special
place.

This book will show you all kinds of **homes**.

All kinds of homes

What kind of home do you live in?

⬆ Joe lives in a house
with a big garden
to play in.

⬆ Katie and Ellie are
neighbours. Their houses are
joined together.

➡ James goes up
in a lift to his
home on the
third floor.

Some people have mobile homes. They can take their home wherever they want to go.

Make a collage

Cut out pictures of homes from around the world and make a collage. Look at the shapes and materials they are made from.

Outside

Homes are usually made of **strong** materials.

➡ Bricks, all the same **size** and **shape**, are easy to build with.

Wood is light but strong, and can be painted.

Cement fixes the bricks together like strong glue.

⬆ Glass is a good strong material for windows.

A strong wall

➡ Using some toy bricks, build a wall in this pattern. Tap the **brick** shown here with a pencil. What happens?

TAP

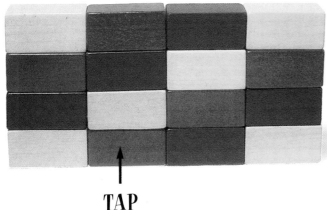

TAP

⬅ Now do the same to a wall in this pattern. Which one makes the **strongest** wall?

Look at the outside of your home. How many different materials and **patterns** can you find?

Roofs

Roofs protect the inside of homes from the weather.

➡ Some roofs **slope** so that rain and snow slide off.

⬅ On flat roofs rain **runs** down a **pipe** to drains below.

Homes in dry places often have flat roofs. Why do you think this is?

Make a mini roof

Roof tiles often overlap like the scales of a fish.

Try this experiment and find out why.

1

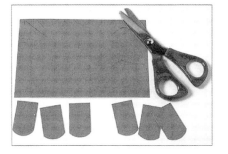
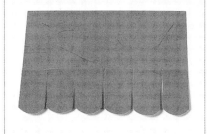

Cut out a rectangle
and some tiles
from some
shiny card.

2

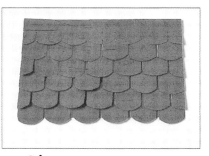

Glue the first
row of tiles along the
bottom of
the rectangle.

3

Glue more rows so
that the tiles overlap
each other.

4

Pour water down the tiles like
rain. What happens?

5

Now turn the card
upside down.

Do the same.
What happens now?

Doors

You go **in** and **out** of your home through the front door.

How many **doors** are there inside your home? Is there a door for every **room?**

What **shape** and **size** are the doors in your home? Doors need to be **big** enough for us to walk through easily.

Your front door is very **strong**.
It has a **lock**.
It has a **letterbox** for the post.
It has a **doorbell**.

Some front doors
have a peephole. You can
see who is outside, but
the visitor cannot
see you.

Doors have **handles**.
How do you think these
handles work?

Windows

Why do you think your home has windows?

⬇ This window has a wooden frame. Some window frames are made from plastic.

Curtains are closed to keep the light out when it's time to go to sleep!

You can also put
blinds and shutters
on windows to keep
the light out.

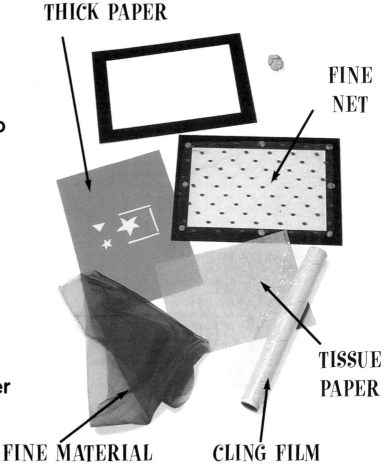

Fun with light
Coverings can change the way light comes through a window.

1 Make a frame from some card.
2 Stick different materials to the frame, one at a time.
3 Hold the frame up to the light at the window.

Which material lets in most light? Which lets in no light? What happens with the other materials?

THICK PAPER

FINE NET

FINE MATERIAL

CLING FILM

TISSUE PAPER

Up and down

Stairs are designed for you to go **up** and **down** between floors.

Most stairs have **banisters** to hold on to, in case you lose your balance.

How many **steps** do your stairs have?

A spiral staircase **curls** round and round.

Do you think a spiral staircase would be *easy* to climb?

A stair-lift carries people who find it difficult to walk up and down stairs.

What other ways can you think of to go up and down floors without stairs?

Inside

What are the **floors** of your home covered with?

⬆ Carpets and rugs make the floor **soft** and **warm**.

⬆ Wood can be polished to make **smooth**, shiny floors.

➡ Tiles on floors and walls are easy to wipe **clean**.

Walls can be $painted$.

You can also use wallpaper and stencils to decorate your **walls** with.

Make your own stencil

1 Cut shapes out of pieces of card.

2 Put your stencil onto some clean paper and sponge on some paint.

3 Lift the stencil carefully and do it again.

21

Furniture

Look at the furniture on these pages.

Where would you put it in your home?

These tables look very different. Which one would you do your homework on?

These shelves could be used to **store** lots of different things. What sort of things would you like to **keep** on the shelves?

eye opener

This chair can be unfolded to make a long chair or even a bed.

Why do you think this chair is a good idea?

Decoration

Millie and James want to decorate their bedrooms in their favourite **colours**.

Which room in your house would your _favourite_ colour suit?

Collect some **coloured** things.
Put them **together** in
different ways to see
which ones match.

Sometimes rooms
can have a theme.
The theme of the
objects here is the
seaside.

Does your **room** have a theme?
Draw some of the things in your room.

25

Temperature

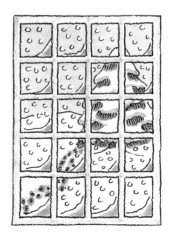

A **well-designed** home keeps you warm in cold weather and cool in hot weather.

When it's **cold**, a **fire** can keep you warm.

Radiators can also keep you **warm**.

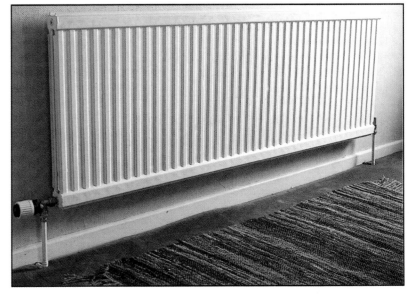

➡ When it's hot, a **breeze** coming through an open window can keep you **cool**.

➡ A **fan** can make a cool breeze when there is no breeze outside.

Bricks, glass and other **materials** help to keep your home warm or cool.

eye *opener*

The Ancient Romans had underfloor heating! Their floors sat on pillars. Hot air from a fire filled the space under the floor and warmed the room above.

Amazing Designs

Look how **imaginative** the designers of these houses and furniture have been!

Outside

These houses have both been designed using **unusual** shapes.

Inside

⬆ These knobs are interesting shapes.

⬆ This kitchen has lots of curves.

◀ This cardboard table and chair are flat when you buy them. You can unfold them and decorate them any way you like.

Index